Sterling was out of position, but he tried to come from behind Peter and stab the ball.

He almost pulled it off.

His foot did hit the ball and knock it away. But at the same time, he hit Peter's leg and knocked him flat.

Sterling didn't have to hear the whistle. He didn't have to hear the referee call for a penalty shot. He already knew he had tripped Peter in the goal area.

And he knew one more thing. Peter didn't miss penalty shots.

Books about the kids from Angel Park:

Angel Park All-Stars
- #1 Making the Team
- #2 Big Base Hit
- #3 Winning Streak
- #4 What a Catch!
- #5 Rookie Star
- #6 Pressure Play
- #7 Line Drive
- #8 Championship Game
- #9 Superstar Team
- #10 Stroke of Luck
- #11 Safe at First
- #12 Up to Bat
- #13 Play-off
- #14 All Together Now

Angel Park Soccer Stars
- #1 Kickoff Time
- #2 Defense!
- #3 Victory Goal
- #4 Psyched!
- #5 Backup Goalie
- #6 Total Soccer

CONTENTS

FROM THE JOURNAL OF

Sensei Garmadon

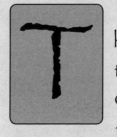T hese are dangerous times for the ninja. One by one, Master Chen has worked to separate the team during his sinister Tournament of Elements. And now, I fear the ultimate showdown is drawing near.

I am glad that I did not believe Lloyd when he first told me he was going fishing with Kai, Cole, and Jay. (He did forget to take his fishing pole, so that wasn't too hard to figure out.) I followed my son to the docks, where he and the ninja were getting ready to board a

ship to Master Chen's island. Right away, I knew that trouble lay ahead.

Master Chen is a dangerous man, not to be trusted. He had invited the ninja to take part in his Tournament of Elements. Chen sent the invitation to all descendants of the Elemental Masters. Each master has a different power, just as Kai is the Master of Fire, Jay is the Master of Lightning, and Cole is the Master of Earth. As the Green Ninja, Lloyd is the Master of Power. And Zane, who sacrificed himself to save Ninjago, was the Master of Ice.

Zane is the reason Lloyd and the others agreed to enter the tournament. Master Chen sent the ninja a mysterious message hinting that Zane is alive and being held prisoner on his island. He said the only way to save Zane was to compete in his tournament. Kai, Lloyd, Cole, and Jay will risk anything to find their friend. I knew that grave danger lay ahead in

their mission. So I joined them on their journey to Chen's island.

At first, Master Chen welcomed us with his usual flair for drama and splendor. The tournament began with a contest. There were Jade Blades hidden in his palace, and the Elemental Master who did not find a Jade Blade would be eliminated.

The first competitor eliminated was Karlof, the Master of Metal. He disappeared through a trapdoor, and Master Chen used his Staff of Elements to steal Karlof's power of metal! That is the real reason behind the tournament. Master Chen wants to steal each warrior's elemental power for his own dark purposes. One by one, the losing competitors are stripped of their powers and sent to work in Chen's secret underground noodle factory.

The ninja knew they could not confront Master Chen until they found Zane. So they

fought to remain in the tournament. But then, Master Chen pit Cole and Jay against each other in a tournament round. Cole purposefully lost to protect Jay. He disappeared through a trapdoor. And his powers will become Chen's as well.

But Cole is strong — stronger than his powers. I am sure that he will find a way out. Well, mostly sure. Master Chen is a devious foe with many strong guards and an army of Anacondrai worshippers who do his bidding. These snake-loving minions seem to have no minds of their own.

And so, the ninja and I are left to wonder: What does Master Chen want with all of the elemental powers? Does it have something to do with the Anacondrai? He sided with them during the Serpentine Wars, which is why he was banished to this island in the first place.

I must do what I can to find out. I hope that Cole can protect himself, and that the other

ninja remain in the tournament until we can determine what Master Chen is up to.

And of course, I hope above all that Zane is indeed still alive. But that, perhaps, may be too much.

As my brother Wu would say, "Do not let hope or regret cloud your judgment." Those are wise words. But I do regret that Master Chen was allowed to create his evil empire here on this island.

And, like my son, I will never stop hoping that Zane is alive.

Chapter 1

n the dark tunnels under Master Chen's palace, a guard with bulging muscles paced down the hallway of the noodle factory. **Purple** tattoos marked his face, and he wore a helmet shaped like a snake's head. Armor with toothlike spikes protected his shoulders, and another purple tattoo — a sinister-looking snake — marked his bare chest. Chains and keys dangled from his waist.

"Lock this place down," Zugu growled to the guard next to him.

A heavy door clanked shut, and the sound of creaking bolts echoed across the factory. There was the **stomping of feet** as Zugu and the guards left. Their shift was over — but the factory workers had to keep on working. If there were no noodles when the guards returned, things would get ugly. Even uglier than Zugu's face.

One of the workers walked over to two flour barrels. He had a short black beard and unusually large hands. It was Karlof, the Master of Metal.

"All clear," Karlof whispered gruffly to the barrels in his thick accent.

Cole popped out of one of the barrels. Traces of the white flour made his black hair look gray. He shook his head to get it off.

Another ninja popped out of the barrel beside him. He wasn't just a ninja — he was a **Nindroid**. A Nindroid with a shiny metal body.

It was Zane!

Cole turned to Zane. He still couldn't believe that he had found his friend, alive, in one of Master Chen's prison cells. Zane had completely rebuilt himself. Now he had a new body of shining titanium metal. His eyes glowed like **burning ice**. He definitely looked different, but Cole knew that inside, it was the same old Zane.

As for Cole, after being eliminated from the tournament and having his powers stolen, he had been sent to work in Chen's noodle factory along with the other tournament losers. But in a stroke of luck, he'd been able to give the guards the slip and find Zane trapped in Chen's palace dungeons. Cole had freed Zane, and the two of them had gone back to **rescue** the other workers.

Cole looked at the group in front of him now:

There was Karlof, the proud Master of Metal. He used to be able to transform his

whole body into powerful steel. He'd had huge metal fists, too. But without his powers, he was just a regular guy.

Then there was Gravis, the Master of Gravity. He had been able to float through the air and make things levitate before his powers were taken away. Now his feet were planted firmly on the ground as he worked the noodle machines.

Bolobo was the Master of Nature. He used to be able to control plants by speaking to them and had been able to make vines spring to life anywhere.

Off to the side was Chamille, the Master of Form. Cole thought Chamille was the most standoffish of all the warriors. She had shocking purple hair and used to be a super-confident shape changer. But losing her powers seemed to have taken the fight out of her.

Ash was the Master of Smoke. Before being eliminated from the tournament, he

had been able to transform into smoke in the blink of an eye. He liked to act tough, too.

And finally there was Tox, the Master of Poison. She talked back with words as stinging as the poison she used to control. But a few days in Chen's noodle factory had taken away most of her zing.

Cole realized that once the fighters had lost their powers, they'd also **lost their mojo**. Their will to fight. That made Cole sad. Even smart-mouthed Ash was a good guy at heart. They needed to work together to find a way to escape and regain their powers!

"Back to our plan to get all of us out of here," Cole told the group confidently.

Zane's eyes lit up brightly, and he projected a hologram into the space between them. The glowing blue lines showed a 3-D map of the underground tunnels of Chen's palace.

"If we all tried to tackle the labyrinth, some of us would get lost," Cole explained. "So

that's not an option. But Zane analyzed the sewer network . . ."

"Sewer network? **Isn't that stinky?**" Karlof interrupted.

"Hey, I'd blast my way out of here if I could, but all of our powers are gone," Cole reminded him.

"The sewer network is old and can only sustain so much weight," Zane explained. "But after adding up all of our combined masses, the pipes will hold by the slimmest of margins. It is a viable escape route."

"Did anyone else understand that?" Karlof asked.

"He means it'll work," Cole said. "Just as long as nobody gains a pound, because then the pipes will break."

As if on cue, Cole's stomach growled. He chuckled nervously. "Not that we need to worry about that."

Suddenly, the clanking of iron bolts inter-rupted them. Cole and Zane jumped back in

the noodle barrels so they wouldn't be spotted, and the other workers quickly pretended to be busy.

A guard shoved someone into the room.

"Get to work," he said gruffly. Then he left and bolted the door again.

Cole climbed out of the barrel and took a look at the new worker. He couldn't believe his eyes. It was their friend, Dareth!

Dareth called himself the **Brown Ninja**, but he had no real ninja skills. He was just a nice guy who had an uncanny way of always messing up the ninja's plans.

"Don't worry, boys, the Brown Ninja is here!" Dareth boasted to all the trapped factory workers. "But before I rescue you, can anyone show me how to make puffy pot stickers? Master Chen is taking them off the menu in his noodle shops, and they're my favorite."

As he spoke, Dareth noticed the two flour-covered ninja staring at him.

"Cole, you're here! And *Zane*?! Is that you? Boy, have you changed!" Dareth gave Zane a huge bear hug.

Karlof looked Dareth up and down.

"It look like Brown Ninja weigh more than one pound," he said. "Lots more."

Everyone sighed. Zane shut down his hologram schematic with a sad **"Game Over"** sound.

"The plan won't work," Cole said. "Back to the drawing board."

Chapter 2

Discouraged, the fighters went back to work making noodles while they tried to think of a new escape plan. Cole and Zane put on workers' uniforms and joined them. Cole stepped in line next to Dareth.

"How'd you get here, anyway?" Cole asked him.

"In Nya's sweet mobile unit," Dareth said. "She made it look like a noodle truck and came to the island to look for you guys. She asked me to be her sidekick."

"She did?" Cole asked. He wasn't sure if he should believe that.

"Yeah, and I was guarding the unit for her when I was captured," Dareth explained. "Somehow they discovered my hidden location."

"'Somehow,'" Cole repeated. He had a feeling the "somehow" might have had something to do with Dareth. Like his tendency to play loud music. "Did they get Nya?" Cole asked, worried.

"I don't know," Dareth admitted. "But if she's not here, she must be okay."

"I hope so," Cole said.

"According to my calculations, Zugu will return in thirteen minutes," Zane interrupted. "If we are to make another plan, we should do it now."

Cole nodded. "Come on, everyone. Let's put our heads together and try to figure this out."

Cole and Zane gathered around a work-table with the other Elemental Masters.

"Why don't we just sneak out of here?" Gravis asked. "The same way Cole and Zane snuck back in."

"There are guards everywhere," Zane said. "Right outside the door."

"Not to mention an enormous snake," Cole added.

Karlof turned pale. **"Snake?"**

"Snake," Zane repeated. "And there are too many of us to leave without being noticed."

"All right, then, so what's the plan?" Ash asked.

Tox pounded her fist on the table. "I say we punch our way out. Make a break for it."

"Master Chen's guards and Anacondrai worshippers have Fang Blades," Zane said. "Our fists would be no match against their Serpentine weapons."

Cole started scribbling on a piece of noodle wrapper.

"How about this?" He showed the paper to everybody.

"Is that . . . **giant egg roll**?" Karlof asked.

"Yeah!" said Cole. "We'll roll ourselves up in giant egg rolls and get shipped out!"

Everyone stared.

"Chance of success — negative thirty percent," Zane calculated.

Cole crumpled up the plan and threw it over his shoulder. "Anyone else have any brilliant ideas?"

"Karlof used to be aeronautical engineer back in Metalonia," Karlof said suddenly.

Everyone turned to look at him.

"Work on Roto Jets." Karlof shrugged. "Just one could take out entire army."

"Great idea," Cole said, "but two things: We don't have a Roto Jet . . . and what good is a jet if we're *underground*?"

Suddenly, Dareth pushed past the group and climbed up on the worktable. He reached toward some pipes up on the ceiling. "Don't mind me," he said. "Carry on whatever important business you are all doing."

"Sure, we were only using the table to hatch our escape," Cole said, annoyed. "Dareth, what *are* you doing?"

"If there isn't a machine that makes puffy pot stickers, by golly, I'm going to make one!" Dareth exclaimed.

Zane's icy blue eyes gleamed. "**That's it!** Dareth, you've solved it!"

"How are puffy pot stickers going to help us?" Cole asked.

"We'll use machine parts to build a jet," Zane said. "Karlof, do you still remember the plans for it?"

Karlof nodded. "Of course."

"Then, it's settled," said Zane. "Karlof will create a blueprint. Everyone else gather whatever spare parts you can."

"But. We're. Underground!" Cole emphasized each word. Didn't anybody understand that jets couldn't fly underground?

Just then, the **creaking** sound of the factory door opening sent everybody scurrying back to the work line. Two guards marched in and trained their eyes on the workers.

Zane and Karlof huddled together at the worktable, pretending to be busy. But they were actually creating the blueprints for the escape jet.

"Karlof can find most parts here in factory," Karlof said. "Noodle press can make turbine. We can use switches and dials from cutting machine. But need more wires. Steel pipes for weapons barrels. And something for rotor."

Zane thought for a moment. "Pixal, could you bring up the blueprint of the tunnels again?"

"Of course," Pixal replied. Pixal was Zane's Nindroid friend. Master Chen had captured

her at the same time as Zane, and sadly, her Nindroid body had been scrapped. But Zane had saved her neural chip and implanted it in his mind. Now Pixal was with him all the time — and her memory banks were loaded with information!

"Bringing up the schematics now," Pixal said.

Zane scanned the blueprint of the tunnels on his internal screen. "There is an exhaust fan here in the factory large enough to work as a rotor," he said.

He nodded up to the metal balcony over-looking the noodle factory. The balcony went all the way around the room, and the guards paced back and forth across it. The exhaust fan was up on the ceiling — and the only way to get to it would be to climb to the balcony.

"The balcony is guarded," Zane said. "We must wait until the guards leave."

"That will be hours from now," Karlof said. "Longer we wait, longer we prisoners here."

"Good point," said Cole. "Then we've just got to find a way to do it without the guards noticing."

Ash, the Master of Smoke, shuffled up to them. "I couldn't help overhearing," he said. "Too bad I don't have my powers. I would create a smoke screen to blind them while we steal it."

"*Hmmmm,*" Cole said thoughtfully. "Maybe you can!"

"Uh . . . do you have smoke in your ears? I just told you, **I have no POWERS**," Ash reminded him.

"But you're still the *Master* of Smoke," Cole pointed out. "You must know a lot about it. For example, as the Master of Earth, I know a lot about rocks. There are igneous rocks and sedimentary rocks and —"

"Yeah, yeah, I get it. You can stop boring me," Ash snapped. He looked around. Despite his sharp attitude, a little spark came to his eye. "You know, you may be right,

though. I *do* know how to make smoke, and how to change its direction, and stuff like that. It wouldn't be hard to create a little distraction-action with some burned noodles and a small cooling fan to direct the smoke."

"Then how about this?" Cole asked. Together, the four warriors whispered their plan. Ash would turn up the cooking heat on the oil to burn the noodles and create a thick, black smoke. Then he would direct it at the guards while Karlof nabbed the ceiling exhaust fan.

A short while later, they were ready to try their plan. Karlof nodded as Ash turned up the heat on the noodle fryer. Then Karlof walked over to where Zane was hiding near the steps leading to the balcony. The steps would take them right to the big exhaust fan.

Across the room, a guard spotted Karlof. **"Back to work!"** the guard barked.

"Yes!" Karlof grunted.

But before the guard knew what was happening, a thick cloud of greasy black smoke blew over to him. The guard started to cough. "What's going on?"

Karlof and Zane quickly went to work. They ran up the stairs through the thick cloud of smoke. Pixal was able to direct Zane since they could barely see a thing. With Pixal's help, Zane led Karlof directly to the fan, and together they deftly unscrewed the bolts attaching it to the ceiling bracket. Cole ran up behind them, ready to help carry the heavy fan.

"Almost got it," Karlof whispered.

Suddenly, they heard the sound of approaching feet coming at them on the balcony. A voice reached their ears through the smoke. "What's going on here?"

It was Zugu! He was back!

Cole's heart pounded quickly. If Zugu caught them, their plan would be over before it started!

Chapter 3

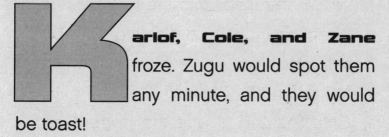

Karlof, Cole, and Zane froze. Zugu would spot them any minute, and they would be toast!

Suddenly, another guard raced up the steps behind them. Like the others, he wore a helmet that looked like a snake's head. But this guard ignored them. He stomped through the smoke and toward Zugu's voice.

"Move along!" he said. "I've got this under control."

To their relief, the guard pushed Zugu and the other guards in the opposite direction.

Cole didn't understand what had happened until the guard who had rescued them came back and lifted up the helmet. It was Chamille, the Master of Form! She winked.

"The coast is clear," she whispered. "Get that fan out of here!"

"Nice work!" Cole told her.

Together, the friends quickly moved the fan down the steps into the main workroom just as the smoke was clearing. One of the noodle machines had a big sheet on it and a sign that read, "Broken."

Cole realized it was the perfect setup! They could stash the gathered parts under the sheet, and Karlof could pretend to "fix" the broken noodle machine. But he would actually be building the jet. And the guards would never notice.

They slipped the exhaust fan underneath the sheet just as Zugu yelled at them from the overhead balcony.

"Hey! Get busy down there!" he ordered.

"Karlof fix broken noodle machine," Karlof said, ducking under the sheet.

"Well, make it snappy," Zugu growled, stomping away.

Cole nodded to Zane, and the two of them ducked down next to the machine.

"That was a close call getting that fan," Cole said. "Good thing Chamille helped us out."

Chamille sidled up to them with a sneaky smile. "Well, I *am* used to being able to take the form of others," she whispered. "I saw one of the guard's uniforms stashed in the corner, and I thought that even though I can't take the form of a guard, I could still look like one!"

"It seems that **we are not POWERLESS**, even without our powers," Zane said.

Then Zugu's voice boomed across the factory. "Workers! It's time for your three-and-a-half-minute daily meal break. Noodle scraps for everyone!"

The workers groaned. But they were all so

hungry, they lined up in front of the guards. Each one got a bowl filled with bits and pieces of broken noodles.

"Freshly swept up from the factory floor," one of the guards said with a laugh. The workers groaned even louder.

Meanwhile, Cole and Zane remained under the sheet, hidden from view. Cole's stomach rumbled loudly. "I'm so hungry that I would eat just about anything scraped up off the floor!" He started to get up.

Zane stopped him. "We must not get too close to the guards. They think we have escaped."

Cole sighed. He peeked out from under the sheet. The workers sat on the floor, munching on their bowls of noodle scraps.

"Man, I could go for a pepperoni pizza," said Chamille. "With extra cheese."

"Or a nice, big salad," said Bolobo.

Karlof looked angry. "Broken noodles are no meal for muscled fighter like Karlof."

Up above, a malevolent gleam came to Zugu's eye. "Time's up! Meal break over!"

"But I've still got some scraps left!" Ash pleaded as a guard snatched the bowl from him and dumped them on the floor. **"Now you don't,"** the guard said with a smug smile.

Karlof came back to the "broken" noodle machine and started taking it apart.

"Many good parts here," Karlof told Cole and Zane quietly. "But still need more wires. And other stuff."

Zane's eyes flashed. "Pixal," he asked, "Can you bring up a retained memory image of the dungeons?"

"Certainly," replied Pixal.

Zane scanned over the images as Pixal brought them up on his internal screen. "There were many spare parts and wires in the prison cells," he said. "We could go get them for you."

"Karlof should go," Karlof said. "Make sure parts are good."

"You're right," Cole agreed. "But how are the three of us going to get past the guards? And won't they notice if Karlof is missing? He doesn't exactly blend into the background."

"Perhaps the **POWERS** of **the powerless** can help us again," said Zane.

Cole looked up at the line of workers. "Got it," he said. He walked up to the Elemental Masters and whispered his plan.

A few minutes later, Chamille had finished stuffing a worker's uniform with scrap paper. She shoved it under the sheet of the broken noodle machine with the legs sticking out.

"See? It looks like Karlof is there, working," she said.

Then Gravis, the Master of Gravity, walked up to them. He pulled a small box out from under his turban.

"I am ready to start the diversion," he said.

Zane scanned the guards as they paced back and forth on the balcony.

"According to my calculations, the time to start the diversion is . . . now!" he said.

Gravis tiptoed over to the balcony. He climbed onto a noodle box. Then he quickly opened up the box and dumped out its contents.

Tiny ball bearings spilled out! The small metal balls rolled across the balcony. The guards didn't see them, and they stepped on them. One by one, they lost their balance and fell down. They began to shout and wave their arms as they tried to get back up.

"zugu go **boom!**" the big sumo wrestler cried. "What is happening?"

Gravis grinned as he silently slipped back down to the main work floor. "The power of gravity at work!" he said quietly.

Chapter 4

Thanks to Gravis's distraction, Cole, Zane, and Karlof were able to sneak away from the noodle factory. They made their way down the dark hallways to the prison cells.

"I still don't get why we're building a jet," Cole said to Zane. "We're *underground.*"

"That is correct," said Zane.

"But jets need to fly! In the air!" Cole flapped his arms like a bird.

"That is also correct," said Zane.

"Aaargh!" cried Cole. "Am I the only one making sense here?"

Walking behind them, Karlof wasn't even listening. His mind was busy running through the jet schematics inside his head. The sooner he could build it, the sooner he could get out of this place. It was so miserable in here! He missed the snow-covered fields and busy metal quarries of Metalonia, his homeland.

The three friends came to a turn in the tunnels. Zane and Cole veered to the left. Karlof was about to follow them when he saw something from the corner of his eye. A light!

Curious, Karlof veered right. *Maybe light is way out*, Karlof thought. *Could be easy escape!*

He was halfway there when he realized that Cole and Zane were not with him.

Karlof should go get them, he thought. But then he looked longingly back at the light. *But first, Karlof see if light is way out.* He moved toward it.

The hall ended in a big, iron gate. But it was cracked open.

"It *is* way out!" Karlof exclaimed quietly. He opened the gate and stepped through.

Over in the other hallway, Cole noticed he and Zane were alone.

"Where's Karlof?" he asked.

Zane turned around. "He appears not to have followed us. I can analyze the dust pattern on the floor to determine his direction."

Cole sighed. "I hope we didn't lose that rusty rascal."

Light shone from Zane's eyes. He scanned the floor as they walked back the other way. When they came to the turn in the tunnel, Zane started down the other path.

"Is that a light down there?" Cole asked.

At the very end of the hallway, he could see a dim red light.

Zane analyzed it. "Yes. **Source unknown.** But Karlof has gone in that direction."

Cole and Zane moved toward the light. It came from a bend at the end of the tunnel.

"Karlof! Are you there?" Cole whispered loudly.

There was no answer.

Cole and Zane went around the bend and saw an open gate. Past it, the light was coming from a heat lamp . . . hanging above an enormous purple snake! The snake's body was almost as wide as the tunnel. It looked very long, too. But it was hard to tell because its body was coiled up, and the snake was sleeping.

Then they saw that something was curled up tightly in the end of the snake's long tail.

It was Karlof!

Chapter 5

Karlof!" Cole whispered urgently. "Are you okay?"

"*Shhhh!*" Karlof warned. "Yes, Karlof okay. But accidentally stepped into snake's tail, and now Karlof is trapped. If we wake snake, then Karlof is dinner!"

Cole turned to Zane. "The other guys and I have seen this snake before," Cole whispered. "It's the second-biggest snake I've ever seen, next to the Great Devourer. It's Clouse's pet."

Clouse, who used dark magic, was Master Chen's right-hand man.

"If we try to free Karlof, the snake will wake up," Zane said.

"**Exactly,**" said Cole. "So what do we do?"

Inside Zane's mind, Pixal scanned the snake's body. "Analysis shows an energy point under the serpent's neck," Pixal told Zane. "If it is pressed, the snake will remain asleep."

Zane repeated the information to Cole. Then Zane projected a hologram from his eyes, showing Cole the exact point on the snake's neck.

"So you mean we've got to *pet* that thing? By its head?" Cole asked in disbelief.

"Not *we*," said Zane. "*You*. I am made of titanium. The cold temperature of my hand might wake the serpent. Once you press the energy point, I can free Karlof."

"Oh, great," Cole said, rolling his eyes.

"Please hurry!" Karlof whispered. "Karlof hate snakes!"

Cole sighed. "Fine."

Pressing his body against the wall, Cole inched slowly toward the snake's head. He held his breath. If the giant creature woke up before he got there, he would be snake food for sure!

Cole reached the snake's head. It was big enough to swallow him, Zane, and Karlof together in one gulp! The snake's eyes were closed. Its thin, red tongue moved in and out of its mouth as it breathed.

Cole shuddered. Then he looked closely at the snake's neck and found the pressure point Zane had showed him — a glistening purple scale. He slowly reached out to touch it . . . and his empty stomach growled!

The **snake** stirred

for a split second! Cole gulped and held his breath. Was he done for?

But the snake's eyes stayed closed. Cole sighed in relief. He knew he couldn't wait any longer. He gently placed his hand to the snake's scale and pressed. Almost instantly,

the snake's breathing grew heavy. Even its thin tongue stopped moving. It was deep in sleep.

Cole looked to Zane and made an "okay" sign with his other hand.

Seeing the sign, Zane quickly went to work. He might have lost his ice powers, but his new titanium body was superstrong. He carefully unwrapped the snake's tail and Karloff slipped out.

"Mission accomplished," Zane told Cole. Cole removed his hand and bolted back toward Zane and Cole.

"Hurry! Before it wakes up!" he hissed.

They left the snake's lair and ran down the hallway toward the prison cells.

Karlof breathed a sigh of relief once they were in the clear.

"Thank you," he said as Zane led them into a cell filled with scrap metal and wires. "Karlof glad to not be big snake's lunch!" Then he handed Cole and Zane two large

flour sacks. "Karlof brought flour sacks to stuff wires and extra parts in."

But Cole wasn't ready to get to work just yet. He looked at Karlof questioningly. "Why did you go down there?" he asked slowly. "Were you trying to leave?"

"No, of course Karlof not leave," the Master of Metal replied.

"Then what were you doing?" Cole asked.

Karlof scratched his beard. "Well, Karlof *think* about leaving."

"But you just said you weren't leaving!" Cole cried.

Karlof nodded. "Cole asked if Karlof was leaving. Cole did not ask if Karlof *think* about leaving. Karlof saw red light and thought maybe was way to escape. For all."

Cole shook his head. "But everyone else is stuck back in the noodle factory! We can't all sneak out at the same time. That's why we need to build the jet. And we need *you* to build it."

Karlof sighed. "Karlof know," he said. "Team needs Karlof. It's just . . . dungeons and noodle factory and no powers get to Karlof. Karlof thought if there was way out in tunnel, maybe escape would be quicker for all."

Zane shook his head. "The current plan is the only potential escape route with a positive success ratio."

"And we need every member of the team for it to work," Cole added. "Without Ash, Gravis, and Chamille, we would not have gotten this far. Let's not disappoint them."

"Karlof not disappoint," Karlof promised.

Working together, they filled the sacks with wires and spare parts. Then they headed back to the noodle factory.

Cole and Zane were used to sneaking in and out already. But now they had Karlof and three heavy sacks with them. Sneaking back in wouldn't be so easy this time. Zane scanned the room.

43

"In five point six seconds, the guard will move ten paces to the right," he calculated. "During those ten paces, we can get back to the noodle machine."

"Got it," said Cole.

Zane counted down. **"Four . . . three . . . two . . . one!"**

Just as Zane had predicted, the guard turned his back and began to walk to the right. Zane, Cole, and Karlof quickly made their way down to the noodle machine. Cole and Zane quietly slipped their sacks under the machine's sheet. Then they got back in line with the workers.

Karlof wasn't thinking. He dropped his heavy sack to the ground.

Clank! The noise rattled through the factory.

The guard's head spun around.

"What was that?" he growled.

Bolobo and Chamille quickly moved in front of the sack so the guard couldn't see it.

"Sounded like thunder!" Bolobo called up.

The guard looked suspicious. "Thunder? Down here?"

"Hey, I used to be the Master of Nature. So I should know," Bolobo reminded him.

The guard shrugged. "**Whatever.** Get back to work."

Karlof nodded to Bolobo and Camille.

"Team help Karlof," he said. "Thank you."

Then he ducked back under the noodle machine.

He had a jet to build.

Chapter 6

Noodles, noodles, every-where, and nothing good to eat," Cole sang as he worked on the factory line. His stomach growled. "How can you stand it, Zane?" he asked his friend. "Not eating, that is."

"I have my own internal power source," Zane reminded him. "I do not need food."

Cole got a dreamy look in his eyes. "But food is *so* good. I could go for a bowl of yummy noodles right now. With cake for dessert. Cake . . ."

"It appears that you are **drooling**," Zane told him.

Cole wiped his mouth. "This is ridiculous. We have got to get out of here."

He lifted the sheet of the noodle machine that Karlof was transforming into a jet.

"How's it going? Are you almost done?" he asked.

"Karlof making progress," the Master of Metal replied. "But cannot figure out how to control fuel output to thrusters. Cannot make work."

"Did you just say something about 'cake'? Because that's what I heard," Cole said.

Zane joined them. "I will run a diagnostic. But it may take some time."

"Did you just say *cake* again?" Cole asked.

"Cole sure he not Master of Cake?" Karlof teased.

Suddenly, they heard a commotion in the factory. Cole and Zane got back in the line.

47

Two guards were pushing four new workers into the factory.

First came Shade, the Master of Shadow. He looked **completely drained**, like he had been on the losing end of a battle with Clouse's dark magic.

Behind him came Mr. Pale, the Master of Light. With his powers gone, he was no longer invisible!

Griffin Turner followed next. He used to act pretty slick, with his mirrored sunglasses and lightning-fast pace. But now the Master of Speed plodded along slowly.

Finally came Neuro, the Master of Mind. Before he lost his powers, he had read the ninja's minds and knew that Master Chen was up to no good. He became one of the first fighters to help the ninja.

"Oh, no," Cole whispered. "Master Chen has all their powers! Thank goodness Kai, Jay, and Lloyd are still out there."

But then Zugu stomped in — pushing Jay in front of him! He set him to work in front of a fortune cookie machine.

"Work," Zugu ordered.

"It's not work if you love what you do," Jay said cheerfully. "The power of positive thinking!"

Cole and Zane looked at each other. They knew what they had to do. They inched their way down the production line until they were right across from Jay.

"Psst," Cole whispered. He lifted the brim of his work hat.

Jay's eyes got wide. "Cole?" Then his eyes got wider. "**Zane?! Is that you?** You look amazing!"

"Not so loud," Cole hissed. "They think we've escaped and don't know we're here."

"Why would you come back?" Jay asked.

"'Cause we're breaking our way out," Cole replied.

49

"Correction — we're *building* our way out," Zane said. He nodded to the sheeted noodle machine.

"They think we're fixing the noodle machine, but we're actually building a Roto Jet," Cole explained.

Jay looked confused. "**A Roto Jet?** But aren't we underground?"

"That's what *I've* been saying!" Cole exclaimed.

Karlof stuck his head out from under the sheet. "What happened to positive thinking?" he asked.

Zugu glared at them from above. "No talking! And hurry up with that noodle machine!" he growled.

They all got back to work. But Cole was full of questions.

"What's happening out there? Where is everybody else?" he asked.

"Nya came to help us," Jay explained. "She spied on Master Chen and Clouse. She

found proof that Master Chen plans to use a spell after he steals everyone's powers."

"A spell?" Cole asked.

"Not sure what it does, but it can't be good," Jay replied. "Master Chen discovered that Nya was spying. He brought us all to the jungle to find her and capture her. But he was really just picking us off one by one. I'm pretty sure that Nya and Lloyd got away."

"What about Kai?" Cole asked.

A dark look crossed Jay's face. "Last I heard, Master Chen is giving him the 'special treatment.'"

"This doesn't sound good," Cole said. "We really need to get out of here!"

"Perhaps Jay can help Karlof with the problem with the Roto Jet," Zane suggested.

"Let me at it!" Jay said. Jay's parents, Ed and Edna, owned a junkyard. Jay had grown up learning how to fix all kinds of machines.

Jay turned to Neuro, who was working next to him. "Cover for me."

Neuro nodded, and shifted his body to block Jay as the Ninja of Lightning joined Karlof at the noodle machine.

"What's the problem, Metal Head?" Jay asked him.

"Karlof made of metal no more," Karlof said with a sigh.

"Oh, right. Sorry," said Jay.

"Problem is here," Karlof said, pointing. "Cannot control fuel output to thrusters."

Jay nodded. "Yeah, that can be tricky. My mom had a problem like that fixing a racing tractor once. She figured it out, though, by using a magnetized output flap. If you've got any iron or nickel that we can magnetize, I can make a switch that'll do the trick."

Karlof frowned. "Nothing magnetic."

"Then we'll just have to find something," Jay said. "There's got to be something in this place."

He joined the line again. "I think I have a solution," he told the others. "But we need

some metal that's magnetized — or a metal that can be magnetized, like iron or nickel."

Zane raised his head. His eyes glowed as he scanned the room. They settled on a medallion — hanging from a chain around Zugu's waist!

"There is the metal we need," Zane said, nodding toward Zugu.

"So, what you're saying is that the one piece of metal we need to escape is chained to a superstrong former sumo wrestler who's guarding us?" Jay asked.

"Yes," answered Zane.

"But **that's impossible!**" Jay cried.

Cole sighed. "I'm never going to get any cake."

Chapter 7

How are we supposed to take on Zugu without our powers?" Jay asked.

"Actually, we figured something out since we've been down here," Cole replied. "Even without our powers, we are not powerless."

"Huh? You sound like Sensei Wu," Jay said.

"I'll take that as a compliment," Cole replied. "And anyway, it just means that we can still get stuff done. Come on, we're building a Roto Jet, aren't we?"

"Okay, it's just" — Jay gazed up at Zugu —

"that guy looks like he could make noodles out of all of us."

Neuro joined the conversation. "He acts scarier than he actually is," said the Master of Mind. "Big guys like that are often making up for a lack of confidence."

"And how do you know that, Nerdo?" Jay asked. "You can't read minds anymore."

"Ah, but you forget, I have read Zugu's mind already." Neuro tapped his forehead. He lowered his voice even more. "He worries that the other guards don't respect him. Also, he misses his mommy."

"This may be just the distraction that we need," Zane remarked.

"So while Neuro **messes with his mind**, how are we supposed to get the medallion?" Jay asked. "We'd need to be invisible to do that."

"Alas, that is true," agreed Mr. Pale.

"Everyone is invisible in the shadows," said Shade. "Although I still don't know why I

should help you guys. As far as I'm concerned, you're all still competition."

"Shade, there is no winning anymore, don't you get it?" Cole asked. "Master Chen tricked us all. You're in the same boat as all of us. We have to work together to stop Master Chen's evil plan."

Shade frowned. "I guess," he said, and he looked thoughtful. "Powers or not, casting shadows is kind of my thing. I can figure out how to cast a shadow next to Zugu while Neuro distracts him."

"Then I'll step into the shadow and grab the medallion!" Mr. Pale said. "I learned to move quietly when I was invisible. Being invisible is no good if your opponent can hear you coming."

"Then I believe we have a plan," said Zane.

Neuro cleared his throat. "**Stand back** and watch the Master of Mind at work."

Neuro bravely stepped off the work line.

"You! Back to work!" Zugu ordered.

"Of course," Neuro said smoothly. "But why are you so tense? Surely you know you command authority. Your underlings treat you with proper respect, don't they?"

Zugu frowned. "Of course they do! Wait — what do you mean? What did you hear?"

Neuro moved toward him. "Nothing specific. But I can see it in your face. You worry about what others think of you."

"How did you — I mean, no! I'm not worried about that!" Zugu insisted.

"It's okay," Neuro said in his calm, steady voice. "You are, after all, a very large and strong man. But do you worry that people respect you just for your muscle and not for your mind?"

Neuro's questions seemed to have caught Zugu off guard. The large sumo warrior nodded. "I have ideas," he said. "Lots of ideas. But Master Chen never listens to them."

Neuro rested his chin in his hand. "Oh, what kind of ideas?"

57

"Well, I came up with the idea for Sushi Sundays," Zugu said. "It would be really good for morale. Who doesn't love sushi?"

"Good question," said Neuro. "Please tell me more."

While Neuro had Zugu's full attention, Shade got busy. First he looked up, studying the lights hanging from the ceiling. Then he grabbed a noodle box.

"Here we go," he said.

He held the box above his head, blocking the light from one of the lamps. It cast a large, dark shadow in front of Mr. Pale.

Mr. Pale swiftly moved into the shadow, inching closer to Zugu. Shade walked a few steps to the right and placed a second box in front of another light. Now the shadow fell directly behind Zugu.

Mr. Pale stepped into the shadow. With a trembling hand, he unhooked the medallion from Zugu's chain.

Zugu frowned. "Is there a bug flying around or something?" he asked.

"No, no," said Neuro. "That's just what happens when you get in touch with your inner feelings. You become more sensitive to the changes around you."

Mr. Pale quietly slipped away. He got back on the work line and gave the medallion to Jay. Then Jay ducked under the sheet of the noodle machine to help Karlof.

Meanwhile, Neuro kept talking to Zugu.

"You're doing a great job here, Mr. Zugu," Neuro said. "Your mommy would be proud of you."

A tear formed in Zugu's eye, and he wiped it away. Then he got angry.

"I don't like being sad," he said. "**Get back to work!**"

"You're making great progress," Neuro said as he backed away. "We should schedule another session sometime soon."

"NOW!" ordered Zugu.

Neuro quickly got back on the work line.

"Very well done," Zane congratulated him.

"Of course," Neuro said. "Now I hope Karlof can get that jet working."

"Me, too," said Cole. He looked up at Zugu. The sumo warrior had headed up the balcony and was deep in conversation with another guard. After a moment, he nodded and stomped down the stairs to the work line.

"Jay, hurry up!" Cole whispered. "Zugu's coming."

Cole and Zane ducked out of the way so Zugu wouldn't see them. Karlof stepped out from under the sheet. He bravely blocked Zugu's path.

"Please, almost done," Karlof said. "Soon noodle machine will be firing on all cylinders."

"No, make it work now," Zugu demanded. "Master Chen wants noodles for the big ceremony."

"What ceremony?" Turner asked.

"You haven't heard?" Zugu laughed menacingly. "Chen captured Sensei Garmadon and that spy girl. He is feeding them to the snake. And he defeated the Green Ninja. Now no one in Ninjago can stop us. Ha-ha!"

Cole looked at Zane.

"We're too late!"

Cole whispered.

Chapter

8

Underneath the sheet, Jay frantically worked to get the jet powered up.

Zugu was still laughing. "Look on the bright side," he said. "At least all your jobs just became permanent. Ha-ha-ha!"

He reached for the sheet over the machine. "Give me that sheet!" he demanded.

Karlof blocked him again.

"There are a few minor kinks," Karlof said.

Zugu pushed Karlof aside. He pulled off the sheet — and found himself face-to-face with the multi-barrel of the Roto Jet!

"That's not a noodle machine!" Zugu yelled.

"That's the kink!" Karlof told him. Then he looked up. *"Now!"*

Cole and Zane jumped out of hiding. Cole landed right in the seat of the Roto Jet. Ready or not, it was go time!

"Cole?!" Zugu thundered. **"He's here?"**

"I would get out of the way if I were you," Zane said.

Cole pressed the trigger on the Roto Jet. Karlof had used water pipes to make the weapons barrels, and he had stocked the pipes with hundreds of metal bolts.

Chuga-chuga-chuga!

Zugu jumped out of the way as Cole unleashed a barrage of bolts! He aimed them at the metal balcony.

Crash! The balcony collapsed, sending the guards flying. The workers cheered.

Cole stared at the trigger in his hand. Who knew the jet would have so much power?

63

"Whoa! Whoa! Easy, tiger," Jay warned.

Zugu stood up and dusted off the rubble. At the same time, they heard a thundering sound as a new wave of guards stampeded into the factory.

"Over there!" Turner yelled, pointing.

The jet was facing the wrong way — but luckily, it was on the wheeled worktable. The Elemental Masters all grabbed hold of the table, swiveling it around. Cole unleashed another warning barrage of bolts in the direction of the guards. They swiftly dove for cover.

The workers cheered again.

"When will it fly?" Cole yelled.

Karlof grabbed his tools and leaped onto the back of the jet.

"It'll fly when it'll fly! No sooner!" he yelled.

"On the other side!" Jay warned.

The workers spun the table around once again. A wave of guards came running in.

Chuga-chuga-chuga! Cole sent a spray of bolts at them. They leaped out of the way.

"We'll run out of bolts trying to fend them off," Cole said. He was starting to sweat. "Make her fly, Karlof, or get her out of here!"

"No problem," Karlof said. "Push red button."

Cole looked down at the dashboard in front of him. A big red button stared up at him, and he pressed it.

Boom! A missile fired from the jet, blowing a huge hole in the wall!

"**Woo-hoo!**" the workers cheered. Bolobo, Neuro, Tox, and all the others began to roll the jet toward the hole.

Cole shook his head. What was the point of making an escape vehicle if it had to be pushed around? "This is why you don't make jets underground, Karlof!" he cried.

"The power of positive thinking!" Jay reminded him.

Cole frowned and kept the multi-barrel trained on the guards so they wouldn't follow.

"So, where are we going?" Turner asked.

Cole remembered Zugu's words. *Chen captured Sensei Garmadon and that spy girl. He is feeding them to the snake.*

"Stay to the right!" he yelled. "We've got a date with a snake!"

Behind him, Karlof turned pale.

"Not there. Karlof go **anywhere but there**," he said.

"We've got to save Sensei Garmadon and Nya!" Cole cried. "Push faster, everybody!"

Grunting, the workers pushed the jet down the hallway. Zane was busy scanning his blueprints.

"Cole, over there." He pointed to a wall. "It's a shortcut to the dungeons!"

Cole pulled the trigger. "Got it!"

Chuga-chuga-chuga! Cole blasted a hole in the stone! Through it, he could see Sensei Garmadon and Nya chained to the wall. And Clouse's giant purple snake slithered toward them, hissing!

Cole squinted, aiming.

Ping! He blasted Nya's chains, freeing her.

Ping! Now Sensei Garmadon was free!

Chuga-chuga-chuga! He blasted the ceiling above the giant snake. It collapsed, showering debris on the snake's head. The blow knocked the serpent out cold.

Amazed, Sensei Garmadon and Nya looked at their free hands. Then they looked at Cole and the Roto Jet.

"Well, hello, Master of Earth," Sensei Garmadon said with a smile.

Jay popped out from behind the jet. "Don't forget Master of Lightning."

Nya ran to them with open arms. Jay and Cole both opened their arms to hug her — but she ran right past them. She wrapped Zane in a hug.

"Zane, you're back!"

she cried.

Zane's head swiveled around to look at his back. "What? What is on my back?"

Nya laughed. Then she spotted a Fang

Blade on the floor. She quickly picked it up and slid it under her belt.

"We've got to hurry," she said. "Master Chen has Lloyd. Once he absorbs Lloyd's powers, he will cast the spell."

"What kind of spell?" Cole asked.

"A spell to transform all of his Anacondrai worshippers into actual Anacondrai," Sensei Garmadon explained. "He is creating an unstoppable army. Ninjago will never survive."

Everyone gasped. Cole turned to look at Karlof behind him.

"Karlof, why isn't this thing off the ground yet?" he asked.

"Two hands can only work so fast," Karlof said as he tinkered with the turbine engines.

"Well, you're gonna fix it, Karlof, 'cause you know why?" Cole asked, and he smiled as Karlof looked up at him.

"Positive thinking!" they both said at once.

Chapter 9

In another part of the underground tunnels, inside Master Chen's Anacondrai Temple, things were happening fast.

Kai held Master Chen's Staff of Elements. Both he and Lloyd had been captured and stripped of their powers. But in a swift sneak attack, Kai had knocked the staff away from Chen and used its incredible power to beat back his guards! Now the crystal on the end of the Staff of Elements glowed ominously. It contained the powers of all the captured Elemental Masters — including Lloyd's Green Ninja powers!

Across the chamber, Lloyd sat slumped, drained, on the stone floor.

Kai turned to him. Taking the staff from Chen should have been a good thing. Except its evil had possessed Kai. He moved toward Lloyd.

"Kai, it holds too much power! Destroy it!" Lloyd pleaded.

Kai glared at Lloyd. He spoke in a low, strange voice.

"No one is taking my staff!" he growled. *"Just a little longer. You had all that power, and now it's my turn!"*

Master Chen and his Anacondrai worshippers watched.

"Yes," Master Chen gloated. **"Embrace the power . . ."**

Suddenly, Kai shook his head. His voice sounded normal again. "What am I saying?" But the evil took hold, and his voice got deep. *"Nothing I don't already feel! I should have been the Green Ninja!"*

Kai pointed the staff at Lloyd. It flared brightly, and the temple began to tremble. Dust started to fall from the ceiling.

"No, Kai, don't!" Lloyd warned.

Rooooooaaaaaaaaaaaar!

The thundering sound of engines filled the temple as the Roto Jet crashed up through the floor! Karlof and Cole sat in the jet's pilot seats.

"Karlof said he would fix!" Karlof said proudly.

The jet hovered in the temple. One of the wings knocked over Kai, and the Staff of Elements fell from his hands.

"Did anyone order some kung pao?" Cole asked over the roar of the engines.

The Elemental Masters and freed noodle workers spilled through the hole. They began to clash with the Anacondrai worshippers. Jay, Sensei Garmadon, and Nya joined them. And last but not least, came Zane!

His titanium body gleamed as he grabbed

a worshipper by the legs and swung him around.

Bam! Bam! Bam! Bam! Zane used the one worshipper to knock down four more worshippers!

Lloyd's eyes lit up. "Zane! Good to see you again, buddy!"

"And it's good to be back," said Zane.

Kai sat up, feeling dazed and confused. But the evil power of the staff had left him. He felt like himself again.

Furious, Master Chen lunged for the Staff of Elements at Kai's feet. But before he could reach it . . .

Shiiiing! Nya expertly hurled a Fang Blade through the air, straight at the crystal.

SMASH! The crystal shattered into a thousand pieces!

"No!" cried Master Chen.

Instantly, brilliant beams of light shot forth from the fractured crystal. Each beam contained an elemental power. And with a

blinding flash, each power returned to its Elemental Master.

Wham! Kai got his fire power.

Wham! Jay got his lightning power.

Wham! Wham! Wham! Earth, ice, poison, shadow, nature ... One by one, all of the Elemental Masters got their powers back.

WHAM! In an extra-powerful burst, Karlof got his metal power back. Instantaneously, his whole body turned into metal. Karlof grinned. He clenched his giant metal fist.

"Now bad guys in *big* trouble," he growled.

Kai, Jay, Cole, Zane, and Lloyd formed a circle. They each raised their right hands high. **"Ninjaaaaaago!"** they cheered.

When they saw the Elemental Masters all powered up, the Anacondrai worshippers dropped their weapons and surrendered.

The ninja had done it. They had won!

"It always brings tears to my eyes when I see the old gang back together," Nya said.

73

"We did it!" the Elemental Masters cheered, hugging and celebrating their newly returned powers.

But as the ninja and their friends whooped in celebration, Sensei Garmadon sensed something was wrong. He scanned the room. The Anacondrai worshippers had surrendered . . . but Master Chen and Clouse were nowhere to be seen.

In all the commotion, **they had escaped**.

Working together, the Elemental Masters rounded up all the Anacondrai worshippers throughout Chen's palace. They put them safely under lock and key and led them out into the bright sunshine through the open palace gates.

"Aw yeah, I forgot how good sun feels!" Jay exclaimed, stretching.

"I know. It's like we've been down in those tunnels for ages," Cole said.

"Of course the sun feels awesome," Kai chimed in. "That's because it's made of . . . *fi-yaaa*!"

Meanwhile, Garmadon had searched the entire temple for Master Chen, but couldn't find him.

"No sign of Chen," he reported to the ninja.

"But without the staff, the threat to Ninjago is over, right?" Kai asked.

Sensei Garmadon frowned. "I would hope so. But **Master Chen is a clever man**. We will not be truly safe until he is caught."

Lloyd turned to Cole and Zane. "Thanks for coming to our rescue. Where did you get that jet?"

"Karlof built it out of a noodle machine," Cole answered.

Kai and Lloyd looked surprised.

"No way! How did he do that?" Kai asked.

Karlof stepped forward. "Karlof used to build jets in Metalonia. But could not have done it without the team. Everyone help Karlof."

"Yeah," said Cole. "We figured out that even without our powers, we weren't powerless."

"That sounds like something my brother would say," Sensei Garmadon remarked.

Cole nodded. "Well, it's true."

"But now that we have our powers back," said Kai, "we're stronger than ever! We've got to find Chen."

"And we will," said Cole. **"As a team."** He patted Zane on the back. "Because we're whole again. And if there's one thing I know, it's that there's no stopping us when we work together."

The ninja smiled wider than they had in a long time.

"The team is back!" cried Jay.

They put their hands together.

"NINJAAAAGOOOO!"